Finding Mila

Lost Girl's Book 1

Roxanne Greening

Prologue

Groaning I reach for my phone. "This better be good," I snarl.

Laughter that made my eyes pop open had be grumbling as I sat up.

"Really Barrett? Late night?" his smooth voice only annoyed me more.

"What the fuck do you want Lev?"

I loved him like a brother, but the man like to drive me fucking crazy.

"Tell the bimbo to take a hike," his voice left no room for argument.

Sighing I pull my phone from my ear and reach over gently nudging the chick from the bar. Vanessa? I think her name started with a V. Shit!

"Time to go sweetheart," I tell her while giving her another nudge.

Her eyes shot fire at me as she climbs from the bed and angrily gets dressed. Mumbling something about men and there dickish ways.

If she didn't want to be used, she shouldn't go home with men she doesn't know.

The door slams as she flies out of it all the while cussing me out. She knew I wasn't going to ask for her number shit I didn't speak another word after telling her it was time to leave.

"This better be worth that," I tell him with growl of frustration. I've had maybe thirty fucking minutes of sleep.

"I did you a fucking favor and you know it," he laughs.
I grumble as I reach for my jeans. I wasn't going to admit he was right. She looked like a clinger.

"I need you to do a job for the family."

My hand tightens on the phone. "I'm not in the *Family*."
"You're my fucking brother Berrett," his voice is firm.

Lev's family took me in when I was ten and living on the streets. We grew up together. But I chose a different path much to his amusement and frustration. The mafia wasn't for me.

"Lev," I growl.

He's dragging this out. I wanted some fucking sleep.

"I need some sleep I just got back into town, but you already knew that."

"There's a situation brought to my desk but Crow. You remember Crow, right?" he asks as if I could forget.

"You fucking know I do," I snarl. My patience snapping one small thread at a time."

"Tone it the fuck down," he snarls into the phone, and I bite my tongue. He only lets his brothers talk to him that way and I was skating on thin ice.

"There's a fucking situation and I need you and your team to help me fucking clear it up."

He wouldn't call unless it was big. Lev respects my choice and only calls if it's a massive issue and I can only remember it happening once before now.

"What's going on?"

He sighs and I know he's gripping his nose in frustration. It makes me want to laugh.

"Missing women." Two words and my fucking

heart stalls in my chest.

"Tell me."

Another sigh. "There's a member of Crows crew who brought this to his attention. Apparently, this member's old lady was living in a community of sorts with woman forced to be there against their will," his voice is cold and hard. He didn't like this anymore than I did.

"Fuck!"

"They were moved about seven years ago," he pauses "I found them."

"What the fuck are you leaving out Lev?"

"Their called the lost girls. Woman sold into prominent families as wives. I need you to go collect the women and keep them safe."

"Why aren't you handling this?" I'm surprised he isn't this is something I know he can handle so why send me in?

"I'm in the middle of some shit right now and can't fucking focus on their survival."

Rubbing my forehead, I start calculating all the things I was going to need.

"How many women?"

"Six," his voice is low.

My mind wanders I need to find a place to hide them. Food clothes. I need to call in my men. I already know there isn't much time. It's a gut feeling.
"I'm sending Griffin to you. I want each of you to take one of the women and take her into hiding do not keep them together. Do you understand?" the relief was gone in its place was something cold and dark.

A red flag starts waving in my head. "Separate? Why the fuck would we do that?"

"Trust me Berrett it's easier to hide if there are fewer of you," there was slight amusement as he said it.

"When will Griffin be here?"

How long did we have to get shit situated?

"Now." As soon as those words carried over to my end of the line there was a knock at my door. Groaning I walk to the door and open it.

"Were you waiting for me to ask that question?" I snap at Griffin who looks at me like I lost my fucking mind. "You always needed to make some grand entrance."

"Nice to see you to brother," he laughs as he slaps me on the shoulder.

"Griffin has all the details," Lev pauses "Call me if you need anything."

I know he was going to say something else but doesn't. there just silence on the other end., the bastard hung up on me.

"I need to call the guys and tell them to drag their asses here. Anything I need to know before they get here?" I turn to Griffin as I ask.

"This shit has been happening for years," he growls in anger, "I'm headed home with whoever gets saddled with me and you need to go to your safe house."

I nod as I start going through my contacts. Sending out a mass text telling Elijah, Noah, and Jacob Cole to get their asses to my place.

I have a million fucking questions, but I don't want to slow us down asking them. I'll get my answers later.

Chapter 1

Mila

I was property, an item to be sold and bartered. A possession. A wife. Words that now defined my life. When I was eighteen, they came for me. On my birthday no less.

The very minute my age changed they descended like a pack of vultures. Seven minutes after eleven am on august tenth I was no longer Mila a carefree happy undecided girl. I had a new definition.

I was Mila the property. Mila the wife. They had deemed me mentally incompetent. Easier to marry me off and get that marriage licenses signed making it all official and legal.

A piece of paper wasn't enough. They branded me like cattle. Forever burned into my skin. Property of Henry Longstern.

I was now Mila Longstern. Wife to the air of Longstern Resorts. No prenup was necessary. I was going to die Mila Longstern. There was no escape and definitely no divorce.

What better way to ensure the line of succession continued with no divorce scandal and no pesky alimony or asset exchange? Purchase your son's bride. Greedy sick bastards.

If you had asked me what I planned for my life. I would have stumbled and stuttered over words. I was lost in the present the future was an alien concept to me.

That was forever ago. Days like today I was nostalgic, wistful, and so broken. Poor Mila always broken as if that's something new.

I looked in the mirror and swore I could see a broken doll staring back at me. Smooth skin imaged to be marred like my soul.

My life no longer held my voice. They chose every detail of my day. What to wear, what to eat, when I was supposed to sleep. I had no voice. No decisions to make for myself.

Dreams were now fairytales. Laughable and childish. There was a day so long ago my lips would tremble, my chest would shake, my palms would sweat with fear, and my heart would pace at an alarming rate.

Those were the days in the beginning. Almost three years ago now. It took them that long to finally break me. Hope withered, burned, and turned to ash. Blowing away in the wind.

I watched the imaginary smoke and ash of my destruction swirl around me as it was sucked from every dark crevice inside of me. Leaving me so hollow. An empty crisp husk.

Curling my legs under me further I tucked myself tighter into the window seat. My mind wandering.in the early days I prayed for freedom. For the life I was dragged from. All the possibilities the future might have held.

Today I prayed for peace. I no longer wanted the future just the freedom of death. The peace the ever-lasting darkness would bring.

For the life of me I couldn't picture myself as the person in my memories. Like I was remembering someone else's life. She looked similar to me, but there was something missing in her eyes. The cold darkness that lurked in mine.
She was carefree living her life day by day. Always believing there was a future and plenty of time to plan for it.

She enjoyed the breeze in her hair and the sun on her skin. Me? Each breath was agony. Like taking deep breaths filled with sparkling shards of glass.

Every soul blackening moment filled with despair, hopelessness, and the pleas of death.

My fingers subconsciously rub the scars barely visible on my wrists. I made a desperate attempt in the beginning a choice I regretted for a very long time after. I learned a lesson. A very important lesson. Filled with men.

Shudders racked my body as the chill of cold terrifying fear gripped me. My throat almost completely closing in on itself as tears filled my eyes.
It's been a long time since I cried. I thought the ability died a withering death inside of me a long time ago.

My eyes swept over the mirrored surface of the lake. The serenity it showed was a mask. Hiding the truth. The evil that lurked here.

From the outside to a bystander this place looked like a rich person's family vacation location. Filed with friendly neighbors.

It was the same in our community before we were moved here. The lost girls. I was different they moved here a year before the others. I was being punished. The year of solitude was both a blessing and a curse. Henry still came around but not nearly as much. That was the blessing. The solitude of loneliness dragged at what was left of my sanity.

We weren't the first lost girls there have been many lost girls spanning the years. My heart stuttered for a moment. The faces flashing behind my eyes. The faces of the lost and the faces of the ones still here. their eyes glossy in the photos on the mantels. Some cold and detached lost in themselves and others filled with despair and hopelessness.

Rains face came to the forefront. The almost lost girl who escaped. My cold heart warmed at that. I didn't begrudge her, her choice. She wanted to save us. Her heart so full of love that she couldn't contain her need to save the lost.
She didn't know. what she could never understand there was no saving what was already gone.

We've accepted what was. But she never could. Every day we watched her beautiful heart break a little more for us. If I had a heart left it would have cracked with each sad smile and gentle hand squeeze.

We couldn't be mad at her for escaping or for breaking her promise to not get help. She had suffered so much she was just as broken as we were. We all wondered what happened to her. Was she ok? How was that sweet boy of hers? It's been about eight years since we've seen her.

Henry was gearing up for children. He wanted to start soon. He promised a doctor would be by in the next month to examine me. He already took away the birth control I've been on for years. The thought clawed at my insides.
Bringing an innocent life into this world. Having Henry's child would make this nightmare past the point of unbearable.

When he told me, it was time to give him an heir, I had a moment of clarity. I wanted to be a mother. To take care of someone. To love them and have them love me unconditionally. But never here and never with him.

Movement in the tree line close to the house caught my eye. A swift intake of breath that I slowly released. Fear didn't control me anymore. I made my peace with what was. My family didn't miss me. They handed me over with an imaginary bow.

Slowly running my finger over the cold glass pain, I let the loneliness engulf me. I was happy the others were moved here.

After the first year completely alone except when Henry came for a visit. The lost girl's presence here made being trapped in this pristine hell hole all the more bearable.

My mind was playing with me again. I watched as a cameo covered arm rose and a hand covered in a black glove made some gesture. It teased me with this possible freedom.

More movement had my eyes widening and then I was blinking. There was no way I was seeing this. There was no way there were men headed towards the houses.

The houses weren't too far apart. As much as they liked being together, they also liked to watch. Voyeurism was lost on me. Maybe because I never experienced a decent normal sexual experience. But the thought of watching someone get fucked did nothing for me and them watching me didn't get me any closer to enjoying it.

Something sparkled. Turning my head, I looked towards the window I knew Poppy was standing at. Her hand holding a flashlight. She flashed it again. Not that it was very bright in the light of day.

Her arms start waving as if she wasn't sure she had my full attention. Turning my head completely I give her a wave. She starts pointing. She had seen them too.

I give her a thumbs up. She doesn't wait but takes off for another window one that's facing Freya's house. She would start the chain that I should have started. Letting the rest of the lost girls know someone was coming.

They would hide. All but me. I wanted them to kill me. If they weren't here to save us, I wanted the death that their presence might offer.

Maybe our owners sent them to dispose of us. Maybe the learned about us and came to rescue us.

The door creaking open reached my ears. My body tensed as footsteps came closer. A small laugh escaped me as the cameo clothed man came into the room gun raised and eyes dark as coals.

He looked ready to tear apart anyone in his way.
"There's not much here of value I'm afraid," my soft tone still carried in the silent tomb like house.

His dark eyebrow raised as he looked at me. I give him a delicate shrug as if in apology his riches wouldn't be found here.

"If you're here for Henry I hate to disappoint you there as well, but he won't be back until next month. He usually visits every other day but he's waiting for the doctor," I tell him with a small smile. You'd think I was telling him about the color of the sky.

In all honesty I'm not sure why I'm sharing so much. The other eyebrow goes up but other than that no surprise is seen on his face. Actually, there was no real changes to the cold hard face staring back at me.

"Could I ask a favor?" I ask as I turn to him fully still not standing. My jean covered legs dangling from the edge of the seat.
No response. He just stood there staring at me.

I could hear the voices of the others as they came through his earpiece. Not loudly just enough to hear the timber of male voices. I knew he was listening to them and me.

"Listen Joe," I pause as his eyes turn to little slits. "You know GI Joe? The cartoon and action figures?" waving my hand in a never mind gesture I continue. "I just need you to do me a favor, well more like two."

"Are you serious right now?" he growls at me.

I can't help it my lips tilt slightly in a half-hearted grin. "Yeah Mr. GI I'm serious."

He sighed and pinched the bridge of his nose with the hand not currently holding the pistol.

"A strange man enters you house…"

"Not really my house," I interrupt him.

"Besides the point, a stranger with a gun enters the building is that better?" he snaps.

"Actually yes," fighting the laughter something I haven't felt in years.

"And you're asking hm for a favor? Have you lost your fucking mind?"

"Well, it's more like two favors now that I think of it," I shrug.

His eyes get darker, and he looks at me like I might rush him and take a bite.

"Alright ill play along what are those favors?"

Now I do smile. It's a serene smile. "Save my friends."

He nods his head and points at his ear, "Done."

Giving him a nod in return I glance out the window and see Poppy trying to run from an enormous man. Said giant is trying to keep her contained without hurting her.

"And for my other favor," I tell him as I turn back and meet his eyes. "Kill me."

Chapter 2
Barrett

Griffin stares at my team. Particularly Jacob Cole aka JC. I could see it in Griffins eyes he wanted to punch JC in the face. his hand flexed and relaxed repeatedly.

Honestly couldn't blame him. JC like to needle you to death. Looking at each man I snarl, "Get your shit together six fucking women's lives depend on us."

Silence greeted me. Sweet blissful silence. My eyes connected with each man. I wanted then to see how fucking pissed I was that they were playing fucking games.

Griffin scowled at the group frustration set in each line of his face. the man could frown with the best of them. I could see the impact he was having on everyone well everyone but me. something that irked him to no end. I wanted to snicker at the fact he could give me the bone chilling fear he instilled in others.

"We got a call a few weeks ago from Crow about some missing women, normally we don't dabble in this shit, but..." he shrugs as if that says it all.
"Right so we have a mission off the books no pay," I hold up my hand before they could run their mouths about who the fuck knows whether it be the no pay or the no down time.

"These women are being held captive and I sure as shit can't sit by and turn a blind eye," everyone looked on in silence not one protest could be heard thank fuck. this will be the first mission that no one uttered a fucking word of displeasure.

When do we head out?” JC asked in a calm firm voice.

“The women have been captive for years, a community of sick fucks and years of this shit happening. We need to go in and get out silently, each member takes a woman and disappears, no group meetings, no fucking bunking as a team,” Griffins gruff voice fills the silence.

“Keep her safe, once we leave here you will be assigned a female, you are on your own, get her out and disappear I’ll reach out when I know more about what we’re dealing with. Right this minute they are our priority,” I keep my eyes moving from one face to the next.

We all head to separate vehicles. Griffin pauses on the way to his car he was in the lead I was going to be his rear and then the rest would fall into line behind me.

“Lev wants you to call him as soon as you get to your safe house,” he nods before placing a firm hand on my shoulder. “Missed you brother.”

Swallowing the lump in my throat I clear it before responding. "Missed you too and now that we have officially grown vaginas let's get this shit show on the road."

His harsh laugh filled the night as he shook his head and headed towards his blacked-out SUV. Turning the key, I started my truck my eyes going back to Griffin who was opening the door to his rig. He turns to look at me. sticking my head out the vehicle window I wait.

"Lev is also sending in Roman, he'll be meeting us there," he gives me a wave as he climbs into his vehicle and pulls off.

Goddammit I should have been informed of this before we left the fucking apartment. Shit I should have questioned the fucking number. Six women and only five men? Where the hell was my fucking brain.

Lost in the fucking fog. I needed some damn sleep. Roman was a hot head on a good day. The man had absolutely no patience and just about as much finesse as a broom.

Running my hand over my face and then through my short-cropped hair I snarl. Motherfucking shit. Traumatized woman and Roman was a fucking nightmare I didn't need.

Why the hell didn't he send Asher? Because he was punishing me for staying gone too long. Biting back the need to berate myself. I knew damn well that wasn't the case. Lev wouldn't put this type of explosion waiting to happen just to annoy me.

The man was meticulous. He already had all the pieces on the board and an end in sight before we even made a move. Lev knew exactly what was going to happen and planned accordingly.

Stopping the truck, I pull over behind Griffin my men following suit. Keeping enough space to get the fuck out and not have to wait for each person to return.

The plan is to collect our prisoner and hit the damn road. No waiting no helping just get your target and get the fuck out.

Griffin turned to me and waited for me to closer to him. He had spread the map out on the hood of his SUV. Roman appearing on the other side of Griffin and pointing to one of the boxes that was obviously a house.

"This one's mine," he says before giving me a smile. "Missed you man, need to meet up for a beer after the dust settles yeah?"

"More like some shots," I tell him with a laugh.

"Now you're talking," he jokes before pointing to another box. "This one yours." It was a few to the left of his. JC, Noah, and Elijah come wandering over.

"Griffin's is to the right of Barrett's. JC yours is the one next to mine, Noah you'd is between Griffins and JCs for obvious reasons, "He laughs before pointing to the last one it was right next to mine on my right and Griffins left. "Elijah's." Roman looks at each of us before pointing to the lake.

"We are right here directly across from the house a straight line between the lake and them. We chose this location for obvious reasons. The other side of the houses face the road and driveways there is only one way out and no cover. Here we have all of this and worst case the damn lake," he points at a few places on the map showing some of the best vantage points for escape.

"Lev is keeping his finger on the families. Poor bastard," Romans voice held a note of amusement.

My eyes scanned the area my ears perking looking for out of place sounds and finding none.

"Once we move from this location you are on your own, we each have a target it is on you to get your target and get your ass out of there," I inform them as my eyes connected to each man.

"As always it's been good serving with you," I give each of them a solute that is returned by each. My words repeat from each of them as well.

Griffin folds up the map and shoves it into his inside coat pocket. He gives both Roman and me a nod. We all take off together. H=giving hand signals as we go. Once we pass the tree line and head into the houses that's it there is no back up. My hand wraps around the cool metal surface of the doorknob. There's no point in going through the window.

The silence that greeted me was eerie. I felt like I was in a mausoleum. My gut clenched as I made my way through the house checking rooms as I went.

When I finally reached my target, she was laughing quietly. But it was her words at the end that blew me away. When she asked me for two things, I never expected the second one to gut me the way it did.

"Kill me." repeated in my head. Words failed me and my throat bobbed as I fought to swallow. The thought of this beautiful woman dead tore up my insides. We were fucking strangers, but I felt like she was important and for the life of me I couldn't figure out why.

"Come with me and I'll make good on favor number one," I tell her calmly. My voice filled with grit.

Her beautiful blue eyes blinked at me as a smile that said I have you number and I know your pulling my chain. Her finger comes up and taps her chin as her eyes went to the ceiling as if she was thinking about it.

I wanted to laugh but I also wanted to strangle her. We needed to get the fuck out of here.

"We don't have all day babygirl," my voice was impatient, and that endearment came out of nowhere. Not only was it not the time or the place I've never fucking used it before.

With a delicate shrug of her shoulders she looked back out the window over her shoulder and laughed.

"Anything's better then, here right?" I wasn't sure if she was asking me or not, so I kept my mouth shut. I was half tempted to walk over to her and throw her over my shoulder.

Her blue eyes so blue they were almost ice chips met mine as she walked towards me. "If anything happens to those women, I promise you I'll make your life hell," she informs me coolly.

She was a fucking ice princess. Her words dripped with a coldness that would have sent a shiver over a lesser man.

"Let's go." I grab her arm and steer her towards the back door where I came in., she doesn't fight me and doesn't even attempt to slow us down. She was walking just as fast as I was.

"When we get out that door we run. Do you need me to carry you?"

Her snort was delicate as she gives her arm a tug. "Think you can keep up?" she asks.

My eyebrow wings up at her sarcastic tone. I was going to have to keep my pace with hers. Hopefully she wasn't too damn slow.

"Go to the left and around the lake. My truck is parked there."

As we crossed the threshold, she shocked the fuck out of me again as she took off. She was like a fucking elk. Did her feet even though the ground?

Fighting the unwanted surprise, I took off after her and damn near regretted letting her go. It took everything in me to keep her pace not the other way around.

Chapter 3

Mila

The wind felt amazing on my skin as I ran through the leaves and jumped over fallen branches.

Laughter wanted to erupt at the free feeling flowing through my body and the look on the Joe the camo wearing man. His eyes were almost slits as he watched me.

"Was that fast enough?" I couldn't help but
goad him. His jaw flexed as he grinded his
teeth together.
I could tell he wanted to say something but
instead shook his head and pointed to the
passenger seat.

Reaching for the handle I had a moment of
doubt creep in. I was running through the
woods and now climbing into a car of a
complete stranger. Was I crazy? Everything I
was told about stranger danger seemed to
have little baring on what I was doing.

Then I reminded myself of all I lived through
and what I was running from. I had another
bubbling moment of excitement. I knew
wherever I was going it was better than here.

As I opened the door I turned and looked to
my left. There were a few cars. Three in
total. I could see the tire tracks illuminated by
the headlights in the soft dirt infront of camo
Joes truck.

"Fucking Griffin and Roman got their target
and out before I did," he mumbles to himself
as he grips the steering wheel in a death
grip.

His angry eyes swing over to me and through gritted teeth he snaps "Are you going to get in or do I need to pick your ass up and put it in?"
My eyes drop to his hands and something in me stirred. Those large hands on my body? I gulped in a suddenly to large breath and almost choked.

I all but dove into the truck before slamming the door behind me hard enough that I cringed.

"So much for a quiet exit," he snaps as he grabs the shift stick and pulls it from park into drive.

"Yeah well have you heard this beast of a vehicle? Surprised the animals aren't running for their lives. If I was one of them, I would be afraid a t-rex was coming for me," I grumble guilty.

The sudden sound of his laughter filling the truck shocked me. I startled hard and my shoulder bumped into the passenger door almost causing me to bite my damn tongue.

"You're just full of surprises," he says before laughing again.

"Yeah that's me a bag of surprises made just for your enjoyment," I tell him sarcastically only as soon as the words I uttered actually made there way back to me I cringed and turned redder then a bucket fire engine red paint.

"NOT LIKE THAT!" I shout out only to add to my utter embarrassment.

Camo Joe laughed harder. "Promise you babygirl you'll enjoy it more than I would that's a promise," he says in that deep skin caressing voice.

"Whatever you say Camo Joe," I say truing to rile him up and get him off this slightly disturbing conversation.

"Camo Joe?" his tone was surprised and possibly a little insulted. The thought brough a large cat got the cream smile to my lips.

I didn't get what was going on with me. I
lived in this hell for years secluded and used.
Only in the span of maybe thirty minutes I
was flirting, teasing, joking and trying to rile
this man up.
Shouldn't I be in this state of fear? Shock?
Maybe hugging the door trying to keep as
much distance between us as I could?

What I felt though in all of this. Was a chaotic
mess of grief, relief, joy, excitement,
gratitude, and something else that I thought I
would never feel again. Need, a sexual need.
I mean I wasn't ready to jump him and have
my way with him, but I felt this slickness at
the thought of him touching me.

Something inside of me tugged. What the
hell was wrong with me?

Chapter 4

Barrett

I watched the emotions skittle across her face and whatever the equation came out to be she wasn't happy with. She looked like she was going to throw up or maybe stab me.

Instead of worry all I felt was this need to laugh. The moment I laid eyes on this woman I knew she was different. This pull was something I've never felt before.

Disgust filled me. She's been captive, held in that house for a long-time suffering thing's no one should, and I was perving on her and trying to justify that shit.

Someone needed to fucking shoot me. I watched out of the corner of my eyes as her hand shook. Her other hand grabbed a hold of it, and she clenched them together.

"My names Barrett," I tell her with a half-smile. I wasn't going to tell her Camo Joe was growing on me. she had a quick wit and that in itself after everything was remarkable.

Her head whipped around, and her eyes searched my face. "Huh I thought Camo Joe was your name." her lips twitched as she said it.

A small laugh escaped me. shit in the last five minutes I've laughed more then I have in years.

Her eyes cast down but before she turned away completely, I watched her lips curl into a fucking gorgeous smile.

I wanted to ask her name; I was damn near ready to beg for it when she looked back over at me.

Her teeth worried her lower lip as she stared at me. debating weather to share her name or fuck maybe ask me questions. I just hoped that it wasn't the second favor. That shit wasn't happening.

"My names Mila," she tells me with a small smile.

"Suits you," I tell her with a crocked grin.

Her lips lifted into this smile that almost had me swerving into another lane. Fuck she was breathtaking.

"What are you planning to do with me now?" she asks her voice so low I had to strain to hear her.

Reaching over I gently wrap my hand around her wringing ones. She had been twisting them and they were turning pink.

"Keep you safe. Were headed to one of my safe houses," I tell her giving her hand a gentle squeeze. Fuck if the men seen me now, they would be giving me shit for fucking months.

"What about the others?" she asks me her voice getting stronger with that question. Her eyes snap to my face and she looked ready to clobber me.

I wanted to laugh again. I wanted to reach over and kiss those pouty lips of hers. Conflicting emotions swirled inside of me. she was traumatized in ways I know I'll both not know and not understand.

I was a piece of shit for the thoughts that kept circulating in my head. I wanted to touch her. Caress her smooth pale skin. Run my fingers through her golden locks and see if they were as soft as they appeared. Fuck she reminded me of an angel.

"From what I could see a few had already been removed from the house and are also being relocated. The others won't be far behind," I tell her with no hesitation my voice filled with confidence I felt.

"Relocated where? Are we meeting them at your place?" she asks through gritted teeth.

The tone she was using had my eyes leaving the road to focus briefly on her face. why the fuck was she looking at me like I was in need of a good swat upside the head.

"No, not my place. Its safer to keep you separated," I tell her my eyes back on the road.

"NO," she breathed. Her voice wavered. Filled with pain.

"It has to be this way. Trust me babygirl I would be with my men if we could. For some reason we were told to scatter so that's what we're doing, you'll be as allusive as a breeze on a summer day," I tell her my tone going from serious to teasing.

Her eyebrows form a v as she takes in what I said. She wanted to right me on this. Argue and cuss me out.

It was written on the lines of her face but just as quickly as that look came, she shut down her face going smooth. If I hadn't seen it, I wouldn't believe it was ever there.

What the fuck just happened. She just retreated inside of herself. She went back to the iceprincess. I fucking hated it. I wanted that fierce woman back. I wanted her to look at me like she wanted to smack the shit out of me. this, this made something inside me ache. I've never felt this before.

Almost like I was feeling a loss, grief was filling me and making my heart clench. Subconsciously I rubbed the ache where my heart was as if I could wipe it away.

Chapter 5

Mila

I was feeling so many things and none of them good. I preferred the world cold and empty as it has been for years.

The anger and frustration I felt had other things coming to me and I hated it. Pain, fear, disgust, and tendrils of desire.

The word victim swirled through those emotions. Pulling and tugging its way through my walls. Crumbling a little here and there as it beat at me.

I survived the last few years by the sheer will of determination to shut out the world and kill anything inside of me. it made the life I was living bearable.

Barrett was poking my walls and irking me in ways I didn't understand. I have never felt this level of frustration before.

Getting answers were like pulling teeth from a bird.

"I don't want be separated from them we need each other," I mumble more to myself then him.

If they felt even a fraction of what I was they were suffering from whip lash. Our worlds were being torn apart ripping in half like a thin piece of paper.

I didn't know how to feel, react, move, breathe, hell I didn't know if I should follow some of my desires.

I had this horrible urge to reach out and hold his hand. This need came to me when he held mine briefly. The warmth from his calloused fingers slowly dissipated leaving this cold behind.

My fingers twitched and I caught my hand reaching for his more then once since. Clenching my hands into fists I was determined to keep them on my lap.

I didn't want comfort. I didn't want to need his warmth. I sure as hell didn't want these things because it would mean admitting that the last more then a decade happened. That I, Mila was a victim, a statistic, a number.

"I'm sorry angel," his gruff voice was filled with remorse. It that was almost worst. The fact he was losing his tuff fierce nature and toning it down to make me comfortable.

"Don't do that!" I shout.

"Huh?" men they were fucking clueless. I
didn't want his damn pity. I wanted no pity I
wasn't a number on a piece of paper I lived
through some shit and…. I was saved by this
man. My shoulders slumped I was angry at
the world and taking it out on the person who
risked his life in a way to save mine.

My chest clenched as the reality of it all
slowly settled around me. I was captive for
ten years, married to man I hated with every
breath, my life was not mine.

My head lowered. I wanted nothing more
then to cry right now. To let the tears, I
haven't let fall for years spill free as I
mourned the loss of the girl I was and the
decade that was stolen.

I could have been married to someone of my
choosing, have kids, a career, or maybe be a
homemaker. But I wasn't any of those things.

"I'm sorry I should be grateful for what you've
done, I shouldn't be yelling and mentally
threatening to throat punch you," I laugh
lightly as I said the last part.

"Mila," he says gently. So gently it was out of character for the man I only met a today. I wanted to look at him but what was boiling under the surface was confusing and I was freaked out by it.

"Hey," he says quietly. I knew what he was trying to do but I couldn't look at him. I couldn't face all these things.

"Listen you can rant, scream, whatever you need to do, but do me a favor if you plan to throw shit or smack the ever-loving shit out of me refrain from that goal until we get to our location," he says with humor filling his voice.

He wanted to laugh and so did I. It bubbled inside me like a bottle of champagne corked and shaken.

Swallowing I try to fight it back, but it exploded out of me. I laughed so hard I snorted. Just shoot me now.

Camo Joe laughed with me the sound rich and inviting as it mixed with my snorting loud laugh filling the truck cab.

"Thank you," I tell him between deep fortifying breaths. The best breaths of my life. air never tasted so good. Freedom.

"Before getting to the house I'll make a few calls to the others, with a burner so you can hear that the others are safe," he tells me with another gentle squeeze this time on my leg. The warmth of his hand seeped through my jeans. I wanted to reach out and trap his hand where it was holding that feeling to me.

It was over all too soon and we were back to the silence and for once it bothered me more the I wanted to admit.

Chapter 6

Mila

Dozing wasn't a new thing for me. I learned to take small moments where I slept lightly. Its been a ling time since I've done it, but I sank back into the seat of the truck and listed to the sound of the truck tire humming as we cruised along.

Barrett's fingers tapped on the wheel as he drove. The comforting sound of his breathing combined with the other sounds lulled me into a comfort I haven't had in over ten years.

"I know you're awake," his voice fills the quiet forcing me to open my eyes. stretching I groan at the feeling.

"I was about to stop. Figured you might want to make those calls? I have a cooler in the back with some water, a few bottles of pop, and some energy drinks," he removes his right hand from the wheel to point over his shoulder.

Warmth filled me and I give him a sleepy smile. I wasn't sure which one sounded better. I normally didn't get a choice and the panic at picking had me tensing.

It was ridiculous this fear. I should be able to just walk out that door and everything simple like this should be just that simple. But it wasn't nothing about this was simple.

My chest heaved and my skin turned clammy. I felt tears burn my eyes as I struggled with the need to get enough air into my constricting lungs.

My throat felt raw as I fought a war inside myself. Panic had my fingers curling as if to claw at myself.

"Fuck," Barrett growled, and the truck was slowing down as we made our way off the road.

I didn't want us to stop. Not now. But I couldn't get the words past my lips. Nothing escaped except a sob I couldn't swallow.

"Babygirl look at me," his voice was gentle so soft it brought more tears to my eyes. his hands came up and cupped my face.

"Look at me," he pauses as my eyes meet his. "It's okay everything is okay I promise your safe." His words have the opposite effect on me. I cried harder.

"Deep breath, good girl," he praised as I sucked in a lung full of air. It was painful. Like sharp little pins poking my lungs and scrapping my throat. My stomach hurt as if it was twisting inside my body.

Another gulp of painful cold air shocking my lungs had me coughing. Slowly the tears stopped and the pain in my stomach dissipated.

"Thank you," I choked out.

"You feeling better?" his voice was soft.

My cheeks heated as the reality if what just happened washed over me in a wave of embarrassment.

My eyes tried to focus on anything but his face, but I knew I was no wimp, so I forced them to connect with his rich green eyes.

I could see the concern there as well as what looked like pride. My chest swelled. That look helped take away the sting of shame and embarrassment I was feeling.

Want to talk about it? His eyes seemed to ask. Taking a shuddering breath, I debate weather to keep this embarrassment to what it already was. But I knew it was possible for it to happened again and getting it out in the open may help me overcome it.

I wanted to look away as I said this. I knew it would be easier to get the words out, instead I let the words fall out of my mouth before I could swallow them back.

"I didn't know what to do. I haven't had a choice in over a decade. I didn't know what I wanted to drink," I stumble over the words chocking on them.

"Fuck," he says so quietly I almost missed it. His fingers slide over my checks as his hands cup my cheeks.

"There is nothing I can say to erase what was done to you angel, there is also no shame for the fears and moments like this, you are a survivor babygirl, remember that you were a prisoner for years and came out the other side," he leans forward as he finishes pressing his forehead to mine.

My eyes close as I take a shaky breath. We've been on the road that feels like forever.

"We'll be at the house in thirty minutes. I figured this is as a good place to make those calls. I need to send out a text first."

I nod as he tells me this. I know this isn't as easy as phone call. These men were saving our lives and it was risky making these calls.

His fingers fly over the screen of his phone. "What kind of thing would suite your mood? An energy drink to keep you going? A water to help you sleep? A soda pop to keep you here in the now with the option of sleep soon?"

The way it was worded gave me pause. He asked in a way that made it, so I wasn't really making a decision. It was easier to think about what my body needed not what I wanted not really.

"Energy drink would probably add to my already heightened nerves sleep isn't happening anytime soon as it is," I laugh at that and brush my finger over the thigh of my leg drawing little patterns on my jeans. "I haven't had a soda pop as you said for years." Sighing at the reminder of how good the memory told me they were I had this deep yearning for it.

I seriously hope its as good as the memories tell me they were honestly I wasn't sure how I would take it if they weren't.

He slips his phone back into his pocket as he reaches for the door handle. "I'll grab us both a drink and be right back."

I give him a small smile and a quick nod.

Chapter 7

Barrett

That was fucking painful to watch. Anger burned through my veins like lava as I forced myself from the vehicle.

I have no fucking clue why I'm more emotionally invested in her. I've never had a woman burrow under my skin the way she does, and I've only known her a few hours.

Those striking blue eyes of hers sucked you in like the ocean's waves tugging you under and trying to keep you.

The buzzing in my pocket pulled me from the confusion.

Crazy ass target is in my vehicle probably contemplating ripping off my nuts with her teeth -Roman

Target is silently staring out the window while shooting me looks I'm not sure I want to interrupt – Griffin

Target snarled at my and tried to rip a piece of my ass out with her teeth. Ass still whole and Target safe in the passenger seat thank fuck. – JC

Targets hovering so close to the damn door I'm afraid she's going to fall out. – Noah

Target threatened to rip my throat out with her teeth if I tried anything, targets unharmed, I may or may not need my ear stitched. Honestly haven't checked to make sure she didn't tear it off my head completely -Elijah

Laughter erupted from me. fuck mine only threatened to throat punch me. my eyes go to the window in the back of the pickup truck. I could see her blonde head facing forward.

Grabbing both drinks from the cooler I close it and secure it to the bed of the truck with the ratchet strap.

As I opened the truck door her eyes jump from the front of the windshield and latch onto my face.

"Have you heard from them?" she asks her voice hinting at her excitement.

"Yeah and I've got to say babygirl I'm thankful as fuck it's you that ended up with me," I tell her with a shake of my head.

Her eyes fill with humor. Her lips curve into a breathtaking smile. She knows exactly what I was referring to the vixen.

The dancing humor in her eyes made them brighter. "I don't need to talk to them now," she tells me with a bell like laugh.

Handing her the cold plastic bottle coated in water from the melted ice from the cooler. I pop the tab on mine before taking a long deep pull.

Placing the cold can into the cup holder I give her a crocked grin and ask her "Are you sure?"

She gives me a blinding smile and nods. She was giving me the trust I thought I was going to have to fight for. Fuck this woman blew me away.

"Yeah, I mean if you told me you wanted to trade, I would know something was up. The rest of the lost girls have been learning how to keep their backbone, it was in a book one of the others found," she nods in all seriousness.

I resisted the urge to gape at her and demand the name whatever the crazy ass book was. Shit this was funnier than I originally thought.

Her smile slips a little. "I've been a lost girl the longest, some of them suffered more then others," she whispers towards the end.

Reaching over I place a finger under her chin and gently nudge her head back up so her eyes meet mine.

"Listen babygirl it doesn't matter who was their the longest or who suffered the most. All of you have been abused in unspeakable ways. Every single one of you have been taken and forced into this life. You have every right to acknowledge that. Don't let it define you," I tell her firmly.

I see a beautiful woman, a strong, resilient, intelligent, fiercely loyal and protective woman. Own that okay," leaning forward I kiss her forehead and release her right after.

Pulling my phone back out I shoot off a quick text before powering it down.

Radio silence revert to burner for future needs -Berrett

Placing the key back into the ignition I start the truck and quickly pull back out on the deserted road.

The rest of the drive was in silence and I worried like a woman that I pushed to far. The thought was eating at me.

Looking in the mirrors I try to keep my focus in our surroundings making sure no one was following us.

As we pull up to the cabin, I feel some of the stress that's been pulling the muscles in my body tight enough that they hurt relax.

This was my safe harbor and hopefully would now be hers.

Opening my door, I resist the need to look at her. I need to lock this shit down. Neither of us need what keeps surfacing.

Chapter 8

Mila

I wanted to dive out of this truck and take off running. My breath caught in my throat as I take in the beauty around me.

The silence was one of peace. Real peace no fear no worry just calm blissful silence. This was why I begged for death. I wanted this serenity.

"Stay here I need to check the house. If I'm not back in five minutes get in that truck and get the fuck out of here. call Griffin he's a contact in my phone that's sitting in the console," he nods he head towards the truck.

I watch as his arms cross the muscles contracting tightening swallowing, I look up at him his face leaving no room to argue. His eyes though they held a hint of amusement. He caught me admiring his strong arms. Shaking my head to the truck as butterflies erupt in my stomach.

Barrett turns towards the house. His muscular shoulders stretched tight in his camo long sleeve shirt.

There was a faint golden light. A crack between the dark ground and the black sky. The sun was rising. A new dawn. A new day.

Camo Joe slowly disappeared into the house and I was left to chew on my lower lip as excitement and fear waged a war inside of me.

The thought of being stuck in this little cabin that looked like it had maybe one bedroom, and this need slowly making itself known was tearing me in two.

I wanted this man and it terrified me. I've only ever been with Henry. I never desired him, so this was all so foreign to me.

I could tell Berrett wanted me just as much as I wanted him, but I also knew the man wouldn't go that far with me.

He still sees me as some victim. I didn't want to be a victim. I wanted to be a free woman. Able to do whatever she wants with whoever she wants.

The real question though was, was I ready for that?

No, no I wasn't.

Chapter 9

Barrett

Thank fuck we made it here. I couldn't take another moment in that truck. Her warm orange and vanilla scent filled the small cab making every breath filled with her.

My dick was hard and I wanted nothing more then to pull her from the truck turn her so her face was pressed into the seat her ass on display and thrust every fucking inch of my dick into her tight pussy.

The thought made me sick. She was probably fucked in the head. So, traumatized she didn't know what she wanted. I seen the way she would look at me. her eyes heated her tongue brushing her bottom lip.

I watched as she pressed her thighs together squeezing them and her nipples were hard little points pressing against the thin fabric of her skintight rich purple tank top.

So many times, I wanted to tell her to button up her purple flannel long sleeve shirt. Anything to cover her even more.

She didn't know what she did to me, and I thanked my lucky stars for that. Shit I could see the war being waged inside her head.

Fear would briefly cross her face, chased by confusion. Chasing away the desire I could easily read there.

Telling her I needed to check the cabin was a fucking lie. I would know the moment someone stepped within five miles of the sides and back of the house and one mile of the front.

I had motion, heat, and sound sensors in the cabin and the surrounding woods heled the same. Except for sound.

My feet quietly hit the stairs as I climbed them. Every muscle in my body was stretched taught as I made my way to the door.

She had me twisted in fucking knots. I was feeling like a fifteen-year-old boy with his first crush.

Pulling the key from my pocket before placing it into the lock of the thick wood door I twist and push it open.

The air that greeted me was clean not stale. I was out here the day I got back something I was fucking thankful for.

The fridge was stocked, and the air was turned on to keep the place a comfortable seventy degrees.

Reaching the panel, I turn off the system keeping the outside perimeters on. I leave the lights off as I make my way through the open concept cabin. There was only one bed and it was a loft bed. The couch was the only other thing that could be considered a bed.

I should have built more fucking rooms. For the first time I was frustrated with my space. She would get the loft and I would take the couch but there would be no door between us. No walls would separate us. There would be no escaping her sweet scent.

"I just realized something. I don't have any clothes."

Chapter 10

Mila

He whirled on my and even in the dark of the room I could see the anger on his face. I know I should have stayed in the truck, but I didn't want him to see me as a victim anymore and if I'm being honest with myself, I didn't want to be told what to do anymore.

"I told you to stay in the truck," he growls at me.

"And I did, then I didn't," I tell him with a shrug. Something in me clenched at my rebellion but I squashed it down.

Another growl escaped his lips as his hands rested on his hips. He looked ready to throttle me.

The thought made me want to giggle. Me the cold unfeeling Mila was feeling. Something I didn't think I would ever do, or hell want to do again.

In the span of a few hours he melted me like hot water on an ice cube, it should be embarrassing really that I was won over so quickly.

Shouldn't I be meeker? Beat down? Was I so broken that I was ready to jump off the deep end? I should be cowering away somewhere hiding from this man and the world in general/ aren't those normal reactions?

The world would say that I should be doing exactly that. That I should be scared, I shouldn't want to touch this man or have him touch me after years of abuse.

What society deemed appropriate I was throwing out the window at what could be considered warp speed.

I didn't want them to keep taking from me. the control over my life needed to stop now. If I did all those things, I was letting them win and I wasn't letting them steel another moment of my life.

I took one step towards my Camo Joe then another. By the fourth step he was retreating, and I was still advancing.

When we made it a dozen or so steps, I stopped. He kept trying to keep the distance when I wanted nothing more then to be so close air couldn't pass through us.

Shame filled me as I realized I was cornering him and trying to force his attention. A small dose of self-loathing.

Broken Mila. Trying so hard to not be the victim she couldn't read the signs slapping her upside the head.

Swallowing a lump, the size of earth and damn near chocking on it I look anywhere but at him.

"I think I need to get some sleep. Can you tell me our sleeping arrangements," my voice was quiet but steady something I praised myself on.

Barrett exhaled as if in relief and nodded to me.

"I think we could both use some rest, you get the bed," he pointed to a set of spiral stairs leading upstairs. "I'll take the couch."

I looked to the shadowy shape of the couch and instantly felt terrible. His large frame wouldn't fit.

"I should take the couch," I mutter as I turn towards it.

"No," his voice was harsh and strong like a whip cracking through the air.

"I'm sorry," I instantly reply as my shoulders rounded up to my ears in defensive protective gesture.

Then realized what I was doing, and anger fills me not at him. Self-loathing rose inside of me. gritting my teeth, I straighten my spine. Back bone Mila. Your stronger than this. They did not break you.

"Don't be an idiot you're like a fucking bemouth compared to me and that couch would like a torture device for you!" I snarl.

I don't wait for a reply I turn on my heel and march with load slams of my feet over to the couch.

I drop down into the middle absolutely no grace and instantly use my right foot to peel my left shoe off and kick it no giving a fly pig where it landed.

It hit something with an audible thud and something in me got perverse pleasure from it so much, so I repeated the process.

Barrett remained silent. Not moving for where he was standing a few moments ago. I could see him out of the corner of my eye.

Reaching behind me I grab the soft throw blanket I could see the outline of that was draped over the back of the couch.

With no finesse I fall over onto my right side. Tucking my feet up onto the couch i toss the blanket a few times up in the air until I was covered then quietly curled into the fetal position.

I completely pretended the man wasn't there. If he wanted me off this couch, he would need to come over here and make me and I sure as hell wasn't going to make it easy for him.

Barrett the asshole saved my life the least I could do was make our living arrangements a little more comfortable until god knew when we would go our separate ways.

Something painful and dark twisted inside of me at the thought of him leaving me behind and moving on with his life.

It felt wrong picturing him without me. absolute absurd that I felt this way. I barley knew the man. I mean good lord there were moments I wanted to smack the shit out of him and then kiss the hell out of him.

He had me spinning in mental circles. One minute I wanted to curl up in those arms, another I was freaked out about that desire, then in the next breath I wanted nothing more than to strangle him.

With another sigh I heard him turn and head towards the stairs. Not that I could see him with my eyes tightly shut. But I could hear his feet getting further and further away. Then the sound of hard rubber hitting metal as he climbed them.

I don't know when sleep swallowed me. it crept up on me like a ninja with chloroform.

Chapter 11

Barrett

The woman infuriated me. Fuck at first, I felt like I was prey being stocked and the next moment she was acting like she was going to rip off my arm and beat me with it.

I could argue with her about sleeping on the couch, but I didn't want to be the prick that stole her choice away. Still the thought of her sleeping on the couch rubbed me the wrong way.

The perimeter was secure. The house was locked up. I would make my way to the truck for our supplies as soon as she went to sleep.

As I climbed the stairs I watch as she curls further in on herself. As if she wanted to be as small as possible.

Watching her felt like someone was sinking a blade in my gut and giving it a spin. Fucking torture.

Pulling out the other burner I send a text off to Lev.

Secure. At haven. Need to do a supply run.

That's all I needed to say. Lev would know exactly what I was saying. Sighing I toss the device onto the quilted bed spread before running my fingers through my hair.

Sanity wasn't going to be something I walked away with after this if the last few hours were anything to go by.

My thoughts run back to the moment in the kitchen when she was stepping closer to me. hunting me in a way.

The way her breathes would hitch and deepen. The way her chest rose and fell more rapidly.

My dick had gone fucking hard. So hard it was painful. That woman was fucking sin and desire walking on two shapely legs.

Reaching down I adjusted my cock as images of her naked and spread out for me filled my head. Her perky tits bouncing as I slammed into her over and over.

Fuck! grabbing my hair I give a hard tug. The pain forcing the thoughts from my head. Taking a deep breath, I slow my breathing and try to calm mt racing heart.

Below I could hear her even breathing letting me know she slept. I wasn't going to wait until tomorrow to get her clothes.

While she rested, I was going to make a run into town. The less she's seen about the better.

Slowly I made my way through the cabin. Using every skill, I've learned on stealth to sneak out.

I felt like a teen sneaking out of my parents to go to a party or to go meet up with girl for a ride in the backseat of my car.

Before I leave the cabin, I grab one of her shoes and the flannel she tossed onto the floor.

I guessed the size of her pants, panties, and her bra. Remembering the way her body looked helped me narrow down what I needed.

The door closed with a soft click. Sending out a prayer to whoever was listening I make my way to the truck.

I didn't need her waking up while I was gone. With luck I would be back here before she woke up.

Chapter 12

Mila

The silence was back. It dripped into my subcontinua and had the unwanted fear that Barrett was a dream. That I was still in the house by the lake.

I knew I was alone before my eyes opened. A painful yurning tore a gaping hole in my chest.

I wanted to go back to the dream if that's what it was. I didn't want it to be, but I didn't want to wake up where I've been for the last nine years.

Then I heard it. A thump. My chest constricted for a moment and then I heard it again.

Tossing the blanket aside I open my eyes. relief hit me so hard I felt dizzy. I was in Camo Joes cabin. It wasn't a dream.

The thump sounded again and my eyes dart to the window over the kitchen sink. Slowly I make my way over to it.

Barrett had his arms raised before lowering them. I watch as his arms flex and the ax slices through the wood with a resounding thump.

There was a pile of wood that he was neatly stacking. My eyes drifted back to his arms before looking at his profile.

Good god he was gorgeous. Tanned skin glistened with sweat in the light, corded muscles flexing and bunching as he swung th eax. His shirt stretched impossibly tight over his broad shoulders and muscular chest.

I felt myself swallow tightly as my eyes strayed to the junction of his thighs. Turning away I walk towards the only door in the room besides the front and back doors.

I had to pee. My bladder was so full I was sure my eyes were almost floating out of my head.

Once I finished my business. I wash my hands and make my way back to the kitchen. I would make breakfast. We both needed to eat, and I wanted to do something nice for the man who turned my whole world on its head. Definitely not in a bad way.

Grabbing some eggs, bacon, and frozen hash browns I set out working on wipping up a delious breakfast I chose to eat.

Then it hit me. I chose this food. I reached on and picked out what I was going to cook and then im going to eat it.

There was nothing written on the fridge saying what I was to have today. There was no calendar of what I was going to do that day. What exercises I needed to do.

Everything was my choice. My eyes look down well except for my clothing choice anyway. But I wouldn't let that bring me down. Nope not when I was tasting this new freedom.

The door opening and closing ripped me from my thoughts. The sound of his boats hitting the floor had butterflies erupting in my stomach.

"Something smells good," his gruff voice filled the quiet space sending shivers down my spine.

"Thank you," I tell him as I spin and give him a big smile.

The corner of his eyes crinkle as his smile fills his face.

"Someones feeling better this morning," he tells me with a quiet laugh.

My cheeks brighten as I remember my little hissy fit from last night.

"Well the couch is surprisingly comfortable," I mumble.

His laugh filled the air and ym cheeks heated more. I wouldn't admit that me being here was what made me so happy. I also wouldn't admit that his bed sounded way better then it should as long as he was in it.

"Got you a few things," he tells me pointing to the kitchen table.

I look over at the clothes carefully stacked up. Walking over to them I count five pairs of jeans, seven shirts, two pairs of shoes, a stack of maybe five or six sets of pajama pant and tank top sets and a bag filled with lacey underwear and bras.

Holding up the bag I turn to him with one eyebrow raised. His cheeks turn a slight shade of pink and I almost lost it at the sight.

"The sales lady picked them out for you," he tells me while rubbing the back of his neck.

I couldn't help it I burst out laughing. Until it occurred to me, they were all my size. I look at the clothes before turning back to him with narrowed eyes.

"Did you mess with my while I was asleep?"

His eyes widen before they narrow like mine.

"I didn't fucking touch you while you slept I'm not some sick fuck who needs to molest someone in their sleep I get plenty of free passes," he growls before continuing. "I calculated your size buy memory of what you looked like."

I was flattered that he looked at me long enough hard enough to judge my side. Pleasure filled at the thought, but it was quickly drowned out but the green monster of jealousy. It slithered in and took hold of me.

How many free passes? Was he going to accept them after he left me?

Of course, he is you idiot, my mind screamed.

Looking away I gather some pants and undergarments, a shirt and head to the bathroom. I needed a shower to wash away the filth I felt under my skin and the nasty feeling that jealousy was leaving behind.

Chapter 13
Mila

I've been hiding out with Barrett the asshole. Albite hot sexy asshole but still an asshole for a few weeks and we've settled into a routine. A good routine. Only a few things crippled this amazing time I was having with Barrett.

I missed the other lost girls something fierce. I hated that I didn't know how they were doing or when I would see them again.

The other thing. I was Horney as fuck, and he wouldn't touch me. I tired swaying my hips, wearing t-shirts and panties. Bending over. Nothing. Not even a little stirring in his direction.

Yes, he wanted me. I could see the evidence. The hard bulge in his jeans or the way his eyes would track me.

But frustratingly he kept his hands, tongue, his lips, and his giant dick to himself. Well today that would end. I wanted him with a desire that was no painful.

I heard him getting undressed and climbing into bed. I counted to ten after the light went out and then it was a silent race to get naked.

I didn't think twice about it. I tiptoed up the stairs as silently as a horse running a race. There was no hiding the fact I was coming.

"Mila?" I heard him say before I reached the top of the stairs. I knew why it sounded like a question he was worried.

Well he should be because I was naked and well, I was naked. I knew the moment he caught sight of me. the indrawn breath followed by a quiet groan and possibly growl.

"Babygirl…."

My hands clench into fists. I was all but throwing myself at him. I was naked for fuck sakes and he was going to send me downstairs. My shoulders rounded as humiliation filled me.

"Fuck!" was all I heard before he was hands were on me, I didn't hear him move. Not even a whisper of sound.

His lips pressed against the back of my neck sending shivers of pleasure down my spine. My juices spilled from my slit and down my thighs.

"Are you sure about this babygirl," he whispered against my heated skin.

"God yes," I moan. My thighs squeeze together causing a friction as I tried to get the ache to subside.

Calloused fingers brush over both my nipples giving a gentle flick before one moved down my stomach slowly caressing my clit and forcing a moan from deep within to erupt from my parted lips.

His tongue glided up my neck before he spun me to face him. My protest died on my lips as his crashed down on to mine.

Barrett consumed me. my nipples rubbed deliciously against his hard chest his hands cupped my ass pulling me up his body as I wound my legs around his waist trapping his thick hard throbbing cock against my pussy.

My hips rotated grating on his dick as moans tore from my lips as he kissed my neck groaning against the column of my throat.

Before I could beg him, I was on the bed my legs fell open as he climbed between them.

"I wanted to go slow babygirl but fuck I need you," he growls.

"I don't need slow I need you in me now," I tell him trying to move my hips and get his cock where I needed it. Deep in my pussy.

"You deserve slow."

Ignoring him my hand reaches down wrapping around the thick hard cock my fingers unable to touch he was that big.

Grabbing his dick, I press it against my opening as I raise my hips. His cock presses into me. my body resisting the large intrusion.

With a growl Barrett presses closer forcing his dick into my tight pussy one inch at a time.

I was stretched to the point of almost pain. I wasn't sure I could take all of him. I felt full. So full.

"Halfway there babygirl," he moans as he kisses me.

Halfway? Oh god I had a moment of panic there was no way that monster was going to fit.

"You can take me babygirl," as if he knew what I was thinking. With one hand clenched in my hair forcing my head back the other reached between us and flicked my sensitive clit. My pussy spasmed and clenched begging for more.

"That's it baby take all of me," he growls as he presses into me further and further. His hips retreating only to slam into me harder and faster.

Then finally he was all the way in his hips pressed firmly against mine. His pubic bone rubbing my clit as his monstrous cock rubbed my cervix. A deep throated moan passed my lips at the feel of being so full.

Then he was moving. Hard deep powerful thrusts that had the bed slamming into the wall and his cock battering my womb.

Each return thrust had him hitting a spot that send sparks of pleasure coursing through my veins.

My hands clawed at his back as I my hips rose to meet his. The growls and moans that filled the room mixes with the sounds of fleshing hitting flesh and the wet sounds of our bodies connecting.

My climax was coming, and it was so massive it terrified me. another hard thrust and the feel of his cock throbbing and getting larger set me off. I exploded my pussy clamping down hard over and over on his monster of a dick.

"Feel that babygirl," he groaned as heat filled me. he jerked and thrust again. "Your pussy milking my cock for every drop."

The filthy words had another small explosion going off inside of me. the feel of his come blasting against my womb had my pussy spasming in pleasure.

"Take it babygirl," he moaned as he thrust again pressing as deep inside of me as he could.

When I came back to myself. Barrett's face was pressed into my throat. His hard cock still lodged deep inside of me.

His lips moved over the side of my neck. "You with me babygirl?" his voice was deep.

"Hmmm," I moan as he continued to kiss and lick me.

"Good," was all he said before he started thrusting again. Taking me hard and deep. The bed shaking as he drilled me into the mattress.

Barrett fucked me over and over again. I knew tomorrow I wouldn't be able to walk without feeling this delicious ache between my thighs. The thought sent me spiraling into another climax.

"Fuck he groaned as he came inside me for the fifth time.

As his arms wrapped my up and pulled me to his chest, I knew this was where I belonged. I never wanted to leave.

Chapter 14
Barrett

My phone buzzed on the nightstand. Slowly disengaging myself from Mila I reach for it. Frowning down at the screen as I read the message.

Bring her to the house. – Lev

Fuck that. I wasn't taking her anywhere her fucked up husband or his family might see her.

I text him back.

Why?

Because we have some shit to go over. –
Lev

He wasn't going to budge on this. Standing I
grab my boxers as I walk to the stairs. Fuck
texting, I was going to fucking call him.

Looking at the bed I make my way down the
stairs running my hand through my hair as I
went.

I could feel our time together running out. It
was ticking down. We stayed in bed the last
four days fucking each other's brains out.

I couldn't get enough of her. The feel of her
curled into my chest as we slept, the way her
lips felt against mine, her pussy milking me
for every fucking drop of my seed.

Just like that I was hard again. My dick
straining against my boxers fighting to get
out and sink into her hot tight pussy.

Taking a deep breath, I release it through my
nose before dialing levs number.

"I don't have time for fucking games Barrett bring her to the house," he snaps into the line.

"Why the fuck do I need to bring her in so bad?" my gut was sinking. I didn't like this.

"She needs to sign some shit and be seen in public for a few short weeks. Exspsally at a certain time of day on a certain day she needs to be seen in a public setting," he growls.

He fucking hated answering to me. I wasn't one of his men, so I didn't take fuck orders from him.

His words penetrated the anger fueling me. he was going to kill the Longsterns.

"When do we need to be there?" I sigh. There was no getting out of this.

"Three hours. I'll have our lawyer here and ready," he pauses. "You better be here Barrett if I have to send Asher to collect…"

He left the rest unspoken and anger consumed me. my hand tightened on the phone. "I'll fucking be there," I snarled.

"Good," was all he said before hanging up.

I loved him. He was my brother, but this shit was gutting me. I was going to have to walk away.

After Lev killed the Longsterns it would be over she would be safe, and I would return to my life and she would move on with hers.

I needed to make sure she remembered me. that when she moved on with someone else, she compared him to me.

Stalking up the stairs I toss my phone onto the nightstand and strip off my boxers. Mila sat up watching me. her pupils dilating and her breathing short and choppy as desire filled her face.

Walking over to the bed I grab the blanket and rip it off the bed. My hand latched onto her ankle as I drag her down the bed and gently but firmly flip her over and force her face down towards the bed.

Without a word I line my cock up and slam into her. She stretched around my cock fighting to contain me. her pussy clutching at my dick as I thrust into her over and over.

My left hand wraps up in her hair as I pull her head back. My right hand clenched on her hip pulling her into my thrusts over and over.

"This pussy was made to take my cock," I growl as I slam into her harder. I feared I might be to ruff, but her moans get louder with each thrust.

"Yes!" she hisses.

Her admission had my slamming home harder and faster. My cock hitting her cervix hard.

Her fingers massage her clit as she screams out in pleasure. Her orgasm triggering mine. Large hard jets of come shoot out of my dick and the idea of my seed taking root filled my head.

Visions of Mila round with our child, had my coming harder and longer. My body jerked as it unloaded into her pussy.

When it was over, I pressed my forehead to her back. Her sighs of contempment fill the room.

"We need to leave in an hour," I tell her quietly as I pull my still hard cock out of her clenching pussy.

"What?"

Rubbing my eyes with the heels of my palms I tell her. "We need to leave in an hour."

I watch as she rolls over and looks up at me. concern and sadness filling her beautiful blue eyes.

She doesn't say anything. She gives me a quick nod before looking away and climbing from the bed.

My chest tightened as she walked away her shoulders slumped and her head lowered. She looked like an angel with broken wings.

Chapter 15
Mila

Life was cruel and unpredictable. It didn't reason or bend. It came at you weather you were prepared for it or not.

We pulled up to this large foreboding black gate. I swallowed the terror that filled me as we waited for it to open.

Something deep inside didn't want it to open. I kept hopping it was broken and we would give up and head back to the cabin.

My luck as always was terrible. I don't know who I fucked over in a past life, but I hope they could hear how sorry I was. Maybe they would be forgiving and give me a break.

The metal clanged as it disengaged before swinging opening with a bang and then we were on our way up this long driveway.

Men in dark suites stood by the doorway some milling around the building. They watched as we made our way closer.

My fingers tightened on my lap. Squeezing the life out of each other. I didn't want to be here.

"Everything will be okay," Barrett tried to reassure me.

I turned and looked at him. I was sure it was written all over my face. I was calling him a damn liar.

His laugh was quiet and filled the small space. It tried to warm me, but I wouldn't let it lead me into a soft sense of security.

The house seemed to loom darkly infront of me. his hand left the wheel and grabbed mine. Pulling it closer to his lap he gave it a reassuring squeeze.

"This is my brother's house," he informs me quietly.

My eyes leave what I was sure the entrance to hell and latch onto his sincere ones. He was serious it was etched in every line of his face.

Giving what I hoped was a smile I give him a quick nod. That sealed the deal I was going in there even if I would rather walk back to the cabin barefoot.

Barrett swung his door open. No one made a move they didn't even glance reach for what I was sure guns under their jackets.

He made his way to my side of the car. Each step closer to my door had my palms sweating and my chest constricting. I was on the verge of a panic attack. I could feel it trying to swallow me.

My eyes dropped to my lap as I fought to keep my head. This was not how I wanted to meet Barrett's family. I didn't want to be a sobbing sweaty shaking mess.

"Hey angel," his voice was quiet and gentle as his hand cupped the side of my face. his eyes tender as they connected with mine.

"I promise I'll keep you safe, but you will be safer here then anywhere else," his tone was gentile, but it held a certainty that left little argument.

I trusted him. I believed in him. I... I loved him.

Chapter 16

Barrett

Lev sat behind his desk staring at us like a bug trapped under a microscope.

"Nice to meet you Mrs. Longstern," his deep voice rumbled through the room.

I fucking hated that he called her that. She wouldn't be a Longstern much longer if I could help it.

"Thank you?" Mila says in response.

I watch as Levs eyes soften and his lips curl with amusement. He was loving this. He knew we were together. His look when he looked to me said it all.

"I wanted to speak to you Mrs. Longstern before Harold came in," he tells her smoothly.

Her eyebrows vee as she looks at him. "Call me Mila please."

His nod was one of understanding. "Let's get to it shall we," he waved to the chairs infront of his chair.

My hand rested on her lower back as I steered her to one of the chairs. She took the one closer to the window. I took the one closer to the door.

I watched in amusement trying not to laugh as she flopped into the overpriced leather chair.

My eyes dart to Levs to see him also fighting a smile. Mila looked at him definitely. She had that look about her like she was ready to tear into anyone and everything.

"I asked you to come here…" Lev started but Mila cut him off with a scoff. "You demanded I come here."

My chest shook as I fought the laughter wanting to escape. Levs eyes widen briefly.

"Simatic's," he says with a wave of his hand. "As I was saying Mila, you were *summoned here* so that we can go over some important financial paperwork, time is of the essence."

Her face goes blank as her eyes narrow into tiny slits. I had a moment of glee at the prospect of the fiery woman she was turning into came out and put Lev in his place.

"Finical paperwork hmmm?" her tone held the disbelief her face didn't show.

"Let me lay it out for you," Lev says with a quirk of his lips. His fingers steeple before pressing under his chin. His soul focus on Mila.

"Your husband…" he starts only to have Mila scoff again and mutter "That's rich calling him that."

Another smile graced Levs face as he contuned as if she didn't just inturpt. "Has some legal paperwork that he needs you to sign. Starting with adding your name to the bank accounts, all his properties, and his will," he informs her calmly.

Her eyes grow large as soon as he mentions her husband. Mila's eyes dart around the room. Looking for him as if she expected him to jump out from behind a bookshelf and grab her.

"He's not here," I tell her gently.

She swings wild eyes back to me. I could see her warring with herself. Her fear fighting her belief in me.

"No he's not he's actually on his yhaut drinking himself into a stupor," Lev informs us calmly.

"But I don't understand," Mila says looking between Lev and me.

"Your husbands' family is going to have an unfortunate accident soon and well you being his widow will entitle you to everything," Lev gives her a shark like smile.

"I would be painting a bigger target on my back," she sighed and rolled her shoulders. "Does he know I'm gone yet?"

I could hear the faint tremor in her voice at the thought he might know she was missing.

"I've made sure he and the others are occupied," he tells her smoothly.

She nods but doesn't bother asking how.

"I'm going to have Harold brought in and we together will go over all the details of the paperwork, making sure that you understand everything before you sign, the paperwork will be post dated to when you were married," he stops and gives her a long look.

"You will need to be out in public a few times over the next week. Then it will be over," he tells her with a cool smile.

Her eyes dart to mine and I could see the hope shinning back at me. she wanted this to be true. She needed me to reassure her it was.

"It'll be fine babygirl," I promise her.

Turning back to Lev she gives him a nod of approval. Lev pushes a button on his desk and the doors open a moment later. Letting in a tall thin man with wirery glasses and a receding hairline.

"Harold this is Mrs. Longsterin," Lev waved in her direction. "Mrs. Longsterin this is Harold the attorney for the Longsterin family," Lev informs her.

Mila's eyes get larger as she looks at the man then it dawns on her what and who he really was. He was the man that helped steal her life. Her eyes lower into angry slits. Her nostrils flair as her cheeks turn an alarming shade of red.

"Mrs. Longsterin would like to get this paperwork dealt with Harold," Lev informs his coldly while looking at Mila. He was trying to send her a message.

My hand latched onto hers and I gave it a gentle squeeze before pressing my lips to it. Her eyes dart my way and she slowly relax's and pastes on a fake cheerful smile.

She didn't know it but Harold would be dealt with as well but not before everything was taking care of.

When it was over, we retreated to my room. The one that has been mine since forever. I pull her into my arms and hiss her forehead.

"Harold will get what's coming to him babygirl," I promise.

She shudders and holds me tighter. I knew Lev would make sure the man suffered just like the rest of them.

"Let's get some rest, I have a feeling that things are going to get a little chaotic soon," I press another kiss to her forehead then one to her temple before pulling away.

I watch as she removes her clothes and silently climbs into bed. Tonight, I would just hold her as she slept.

Chapter 17

Mila

I wasn't sure how I was supposed to feel. Things were going of kilter again. I thought I just found my place with Barrett in the cabin and now I'm in the city with his brother and so many changes.

For starters I was rich. Well I would be tomorrow according to Lev. I would get a phone call about the unfortunate demise of my husband and his parents.

Harold would inform the police I was away visiting an old relative and give them my phone number to reach me.

Barrett placed his arm over my shoulders as we went from store to store. I was getting better at this. I knew what I wanted to wear and what I wanted to eat when I was hungry.

As we passed a pharmacy it occurred to me, I didn't have any feminine products and then it hit me like a door to the face. I haven't needed any of those products in weeks like to many weeks.

Feeling sick I come to a stop as the implications of it swirl through my chaotic mind.

Barrett comes to a stop with me. he looks down at me with concern. Before he can open his mouth, I blurt out.

"I need to go in there for a few minutes." Pasting on the biggest smile I can muster.

His eyebrows lower as he glances from me to the pharmacy. As if putting two and two together and coming up with womanly

113

problems his face turned an alarming shade of pale white.

"Why don't you wait out here for me?" I ask him sweetly. This worked out for the best one of the things I wanted to buy happened to be something I didn't want him to see. At least not until I knew for sure and only if it was positive.

Giving him a big smile, I turn to the door. Butterflies rushed inside of me as my thoughts churned with the possibilities.

Before meeting Barrett this would have been a crippling moment. This would have been what broken me. but now. Well now I wanted nothing more then that test to show that yes, I was pregnant.

I all but skip through the store with my newfound confidence. Just moments ago, I would have been freaking out and dragging feet. Now. Now that I had a moment to process the possibility, I was excited to the point of giddiness.

The ride back to the house was filled with laughs and smiles. Both mine and Barrett's. I haven't had the courage to tell him how much I loved him. But after I took this test, I would be telling him two very important things I just knew it.

As soon as we reached the house, I rushed for the stairs giggling the whole way. Barrett's chuckles faded behind me.

He was headed to Levs office to go over what was needed tomorrow. That was another thing that made this all the better. Tomorrow I would be free. Free of the Longsterns, of the fear, I would be free to be me.

Whoever thought peeing on a stick without making a mess was easy well fuck off. That shit wasn't even close to being sanitary.

The time it took for it to register was one that seemed to take a lifetime even if it was only a few moments.

My eyes filled with tears that I had to blink back. It said exactly what I wanted it too. I was pregnant with Barrett's child. We were going to have a baby.

Wrapping the stick up I hide it in the bathroom. As much as I wanted to run out there and tell him everything I wanted to wait until I was officially free.

Tomorrow couldn't come soon enough.

Chapter 18

Barrett

It was five minutes to noon when we got the text. Mila was glowing as she sat eating her steak salad.

Her eyes meet mine and without a word she bursts into tears. She knew without having to ask. It was over they were gone.

Getting up from her seat she launched herself at me. pressing kisses to my face as she whispered how much she loved me.

"I love you," she tells me again this time her hands were cupping my cheeks. Her eyes locked on mine.

I sat there staring at the most beautiful woman I have ever met as she declared her love for me.

"Barrett?" she says quietly.

"Yeah?" I ask her. My brain sluggish.

"I'm pregnant," her words were steady and filled with concern.

"Pregnant?" I utter like a fucking parrot.

"Yes," she says slowly as if she wasn't sure if I was mentally okay.

"You love me and you're pregnant with our child?" I stumble over the words.

"Yes," she says more firmly.

My hands cup her face as I pull her closer. Her eyes widen before my lips crash down onto hers.

Fuck I needed her. I needed to fuck her right here right now. But I couldn't we were in a fucking restaurant. Gently I pulled back and peck her lips on more time.

"Let's get the check, unless your still hungry. The baby probably needs the sustenance."

Mila's eyes fill with laughter as the words fly out of my mouth.

"Check, to-go boxes and your truck now," she says as she stands and heads over to her side of the table.

My dick gets harder than it ever has before. Pressing into the zipper of my jeans demanding freedom to push into her tight pussy.

Waving to the waitress who had been trying to get my attention in ways I didn't want made my skin crawl.

She all but tripped over herself to get to our table.

"Yes?" her breathless voice reached my ears.

Taking my eyes off Mila briefly I look up at the brunette. "My fiancée and I would like the check and some to-go boxes," I tell her as my eyes latch onto Mila's face.

I wanted to see her reaction as I inform the lady, she was my fiancée.

Mila's eyes were filled with tears. She was nodding so hard I thought she would get whiplash.

The waitress huffed and stormed off. Not that I gave a shit.

"Are you sure? It's not because of the baby, right?" she asks in concern.

"Babygirl, I'm not asking you because your pregnant I want you to be my wife because I fucking love you," I tell her gruffly.

She smiles that big smile before saying "You're not asking your telling," she points at me as she laughs "But I wouldn't have it any other way."

We don't make it far before I'm pulling the truck over and reaching for her. Mila already removed her panties as I steered the truck off the road.

Her knees were on either side of my thighs as she pulled my cock from my jeans. Her mouth latched onto mine as she slowly lowered herself over my throbbing dick.

Reaching around her I wrap one hand around her shoulder and the other in her hair.

Pulling my lips from hers I tug her hair and force her head back as my lips caress her throat.

My hips thrust up into her over and over cramming ever inch on my thick length into her tight spasming pussy. With each hard thrust I push her down with my hand on her shoulder forcing her to take everything I have to give.

Her throaty moans turn to screams as she orgasms on my dick. Her juices coating my balls and her thighs.

With a grunt I empty myself into her heated clenching depths. If she wasn't already pregnant, she would be now.

The thought made me smile and my cock harden further.

"Again?" she breathed as she rotated her hips.

"Ride me Babygirl," I groan as she does just that. Taking me deep milking me for all I was worth.

When we came again, she slumped against my with a sleepy content smile.

"Let's go home angel," I tell her before pressing a kiss to the top of her head.

"The cabin?" she asks hopefully.

"Yeah babygirl the cabin. We need to stop in and get our stuff and say goodbye to Lev," I tell her as she slowly climbed back over into her seat.

"Good," she smiles and closes her eyes falling into a deep sleep.

What I didn't tell her was that we needed to head out today because Elijah was on his way to Levs tonight and we needed to be missing before him and his target made it to the house.

I wonder how it went with his target. Hopefully as good as it did with mine.

Brushing her hair from her face I steer us towards the house.

It was time to get this show back on the road and this time Mila wasn't my target she was my everything.

Epilogue

I was climbing the fucking walls. Mila wanted a home birth and I wanted her and our baby at the damn hospital with real doctors not some hack.

Mila groaned again as another contraction struck her eyes closing as she gritted her teeth.

"Feel that, that's gods' gifts to us woman," the midwife informed her.

Mila opened her eyes and glared at the women and for a moment I thought id get my way and we would call an ambulance to collect us and take us to proper medical care.

"That doesn't feel like a gift," Mila snapped and snarled.

For a moment the midwifes eyes widened before she shook it off and told her to take a deep breath and release it.

Mila scoffed at the lady. "When your insides are being rearranged and you whoha is being torn apart you can tell me it's a damn gift, right now I want to push so wither help me or get the hell out of the way!" Mila paused before bellowing out. "Barrett!"

"Her wild eyes land on me as I lean closer. "Get down there and get out kid from my whoha!" she snarled at me as she grabbed the collar of my shirt and pulled me closer to her.

I don't argue or even tell her I could call for help. I wanted to live past the next few minutes.

Her hand releases me as she glares at the midwife who was staring back with wide eyes.

"He doesn't know what he's doing," she stutters.

"How fucking hard is it to catch a damn baby? Fucking help him!" Mila shouts out.

The midwife finally seems to have found her brain as she rushed to the foot of the bed.

A few grunting pushes and snarls later and the sound of our daughter screaming into the room filled the air.

"She's perfect Mila," I tell her reverently as I bring her to her mother and place her on her chest.

Our daughter starts rooting around looking for boob electing a laugh from Mila.

I watch as Mila guides her to her breast. Our daughter latching on with a grunt before the room was filled with her suckling sounds.

The mid wife waited for our daughter to finish before scooping her up and giving her a wipe down.

"She's beautiful," I tell my wife.

"She looks just like her daddy," Mila whispers to me with a smile.

Our daughter had my dark hair and Mila's angel like face.

"Arianna may have my dark hair but she has your angelic beauty," I tell her as I press my lips to her forehead.

"I love you," she whispers tearfully.

"I love you too babygirl."

The End.